SNOW

Uri Shulevitz

SQUARE
FISH

Farrar Straus Giroux

SQUARE
FISH

An Imprint of Macmillan

SNOW. Copyright © 1998 by Uri Shulevitz. All rights reserved.
Printed in the United States of America by Phoenix Color Corp. d/b/a Lehigh Rockaway, New Jersey, U.S.A.
For information, address Square Fish, 175 Fifth Avenue, New York, NY 10010.

Square Fish and the Square Fish logo are trademarks of Macmillan and
are used by Farrar Straus Giroux under license from Macmillan.

Library of Congress Cataloging-in-Publication Data
Shulevitz, Uri, 1935–
Snow / Uri Shulevitz.
p. cm.
Summary: As snowflakes slowly come down, one by one, people in
the city ignore them, and only a boy and his dog think that the
snowfall will amount to anything.
ISBN 978-0-374-46862-0
[1. Snow—Fiction. 2. City and town life—Fiction.] I. Title.
PZ7. S5594Sn 1998   [E]—dc21   97037257

Originally published in the United States by Farrar Straus Giroux
First Square Fish Edition: October 2011
Square Fish logo designed by Filomena Tuosto
mackids.com

28 27 26 25 24 23 22 21 20

AR: 1.6 / LEXILE: 220L

*For
Margaret Ferguson*

*and for
Kiddo*

The skies are gray.
The rooftops are gray.
The whole city is gray.

Then

one snowflake.

"It's snowing,"
said boy with dog.

"It's only a snowflake,"
said grandfather with beard.

Then
two snowflakes.
"It's snowing,"
said boy with dog.

"It's nothing,"
said man with hat.

Then
three snowflakes.
"It's snowing," said boy with dog.

"It'll melt," said woman with umbrella.

A few snowflakes float down
and melt.

But as soon as one snowflake melts
another takes its place.

"No snow," said radio.

"No snow,"
said television.

But snowflakes don't listen to radio,

snowflakes don't
watch television.

All snowflakes know
is snow, snow, and snow.

Snowflakes keep coming and coming and coming,

circling and swirling,
spinning and twirling,

dancing, playing,
there, and there,

floating, floating through the air,

falling, falling everywhere.

And rooftops grow lighter,
and lighter.

"It's snowing," said boy with dog.

The rooftops are white.

The whole city is white.

"Snow," said the boy.